DR IBRAHIM SAYUTI

THE RADIANCE OF DUA AZKAR

A COMPREHENSIVE DUA BOOK WITH TRANSLITRATION AND TRANSLATION.

DR IBRAHIM SAYUTI

DR IBRAHIM SAYUTI

INTRODUCTION

Islam's Morning Azkar:

A Source of Spiritual Awakening and Direction

As a form of spiritual awakening, direction, and attentiveness, the morning azkar, or supplications, are of utmost importance in Islam. The azkar for this morning is a collection of recitations that Muslims are advised to perform following the Fajr prayer in the early morning hours. The purpose of this essay is to examine the Islamic practice of morning azkar and its enormous effects on a person's spiritual health from an educational perspective.

1. Thanking Allah and keeping Him in Mind:

Muslims have the chance to thank Allah for blessing them with a fresh day of life and blessings at the morning azkar. People appreciate the divine mercies and bounties bestowed upon them by saying specific invocations such as "Alhamdulillah" (all thanks be to Allah) and "SubhanAllah" (glory be to Allah). These acts of remembering and thankfulness foster humility, contentment, and an awareness of Allah's ongoing protection and direction.

2. Setting the Day's Righteous Intentions:

Muslims can establish good intentions and ask Allah for guidance for their acts and endeavors throughout the day by performing the morning azkar. People can intentionally match their intents and deeds with the teachings of Islam by reciting prayers like "Allahumma inni as'aluka khayra had al-yawm" (O Allah, I beseech You for the kindness of this day). This technique aids people in remaining committed to their pursuit of virtue, asking Allah for guidance in making moral decisions and maintaining their concentration on their spiritual objectives.

3. Seeking Defense Against Evil and Negative Forces

Some invocations during the morning azkar act as a barrier against evil and unfavorable influences. Reciting "A'udhu billahi min ash shaitan Raheemem" (I seek shelter in Allah from Satan, the accursed) makes one more vigilant and resilient as they face the hardships of the day by asking Allah for protection against Satan's whispers and temptations. These supplications stress the necessity for Muslims to seek divine direction to be protected from negative influences and serve as a reminder of the ongoing conflict between good and evil.

4. Building Inner Peace and Mindfulness

By reminding Muslims of their spiritual connection to Allah and the fleeting nature of worldly affairs, morning azkar helps Muslims achieve a state of mindfulness and inner serenity. The recitation of lines like "La ilaha illallah" (There is no god but Allah) and "La hawla wala quwwata illa billah" (There is no might or might except with Allah) aids people in focusing on their spiritual journeys and distancing themselves from worldly distractions. Such reflective and attentive moments result in a rise in serenity, gratitude, and a sense of direction in one's everyday activities.

5. Faith and Strengthening Resilience:

The exercise of morning azkar is essential for enhancing faith and developing fortitude in the face of difficulties. People can strengthen their conviction in the foundational ideas of Islam by reciting invocations that proclaim Allah's Oneness, such as "La ilaha illallah wahdahu la sharika lah" (There is no god but Allah, alone, without companion). This act of affirming one's faith fosters self-assurance, faith in Allah's knowledge, and resiliency in the face of challenges.

6.Setting Up a Spiritual Schedule and Discipline:

A Muslim's daily life is established with morning azkar as a spiritual practise and discipline. They help people stay connected to their Creator by serving as a reminder to start each day with the remembrance of Allah.

ALLAH SAID **And remember your lord in prayer each morning and evening.**

That you (the people) may believe in Allah and His Messenger, revere him, respect the Prophet, and magnify Allah Day and Night.

CHAPTER 1

MORNING AZKAR

1. AL FATIHA (THE OPENING)
RECITE ONCE IN THE MORNING

TRANSLITERATION

1. Bismillaahir Rahmaa-nir Raheem.
2. Alhamdu lillaahi rabbil aa'lameen.
3. Ar-rahmaa nir-raheem.
4. Maaliki'yaw mid-deen.
5. Iyyaa kana'budu wa-lyyaa kanasta'een.
6. Ih'dinas siraa'tal mustaqeem.

7. Siraatal-ladheena an'amta alai'him ghayril maghdoo bi'alai'him wa'lad daal-leen.

TRANSLATION

1. In the name of Allah, the Most Merciful, the Most Compassionate.

2. All praise is due to Allah, the creator of the universe.

3. The Forgiving and the Particularly Forgiving.

4. Ruler of the Day of Restitution.

5. We worship You and seek assistance from You.

6. Lead us along the right road.

7. The way of those You have shown favor to, not the way of those who have incited [Your] wrath or the way of the lost.

DUA 2.

TRANSLITERATION

Bismillaahir Rahmaa-nir Raheem

1 Alif Laam Meem.

2 Dha'likal kitaabu-laa raiba : feeh : hudal-lil muttaqeen.

3 Al-ladhina yu'minoona bil'ghaibi wa-yu'qee-moonas salata wa mim'maa razaqna'hum yun'fiqoon.

4 Wal-ladhina yu'minoona bimaa un'zila ilaika wama un'zila min qablika wa-bil aa'khirati hum yu'qinoon.

5 Ulaa-ika a'laa hudam-mir rabbihim; wa-ulaa-ika humul muf'lihoon.

TRANSLATION

In the name of Allah, the Most Forgiving, the Most Merciful.

Alif-Lam-Mim is 1.

None other than Allah (Alone) is aware of the meanings of these letters, which are one of the wonders of the Qur'an.

2 For those who are aware of Allah, this is the Book about which there is no question.

3 Who establish prayer, have faith in the unseen, and give from what We have given them.

4 And those who have confidence in what has been revealed to you, [O Muhammad], what has been revealed before you, and what will be revealed in the Hereafter.

5 Those who follow their Lord's [correct] direction are the successful ones.

3. AYATU KURSI (THE THRON).

RECITE ONCE IN THE MORING

TRANSLITERATION

Bismillaahir Rahmaa-nir Raheem

Allahu la-ilaaha illaa'hu wal haiyul qai-yoom;

Laa-ta'khudhuhoo sinatu'oo walaa na'woom;

Lahoo ma-fis'samaawaati wama fil ard;

Man dhal'ladhi yashfa'u in'dahoo illa be-idh'nihi;

Ya-lamu ma-baina ai'deehim wama khal-fahum;

Wa-laa yuhee'toona be-shai-im-min il-mihee illa be'maa shaa;

Wasi'aa kursi'yuhus samaa-waati wal arda;

Wa-laa yaoo'duhoo hif'Dhuhumaa wa-huwal ali'yyul adheem.

TRANSLATION

In the name of Allah, the Most Merciful and the Most Compassionate

No other god exists except Allah, the Sustainer of [all] existence and the Ever-Living. He is neither overcome by sleep nor weariness. Both the sky and the earth are His, and they both belong to Him. Who among us has the authority to petition Him without His consent? They do not include anything from His knowledge other than what He wills, even though He knows what is [now] before them and what will come after them. His Kursi encompasses both the heavens and the earth, and He is unwearied in their upkeep. And He is the Greatest and Highest.

DUA 4.

RECITE ONCE IN THE MORING

TRANSLITERATION

Laa ik'raaha fid-deen;

Qat-tabay'yanar rushdu minal ghayy;

Famai yakfur bit-taa'ghooti wa-yu'mim billaahi faqadis tamsaka bil'urwatil wusqaa lan fisaama luhuu;

Walla'hu samee'un aleem.

TRANSLATION

The acceptance of the religion shall not be forced. The correct path has emerged from the incorrect one. Whoever rejects Taghut and adheres to the teachings of Allah has so firmly grasped the most solid handhold. And Allah Hears and Knows.

DUA 5.

RECITE ONCE IN THE MORING

TRANSLITERATION

Allahu wali-yyul ladhina aa'manu yukh'rijuhum minadh-dhulumaati ilan noor;

Wal-ladhi na-kafaroo awliyaa uo'humut taa'ghootu yukh-rijoo'nahum minan noori iladh-dhulumaat;

Ulaa-ika as'haabun naari hum fee-haa khaa'lidoon

TRANSLATION

Those who believe have Allah on their side. He leads them from the shadows and into the sunshine. Taught are the allies of the disbelieving. They transport them into the dark from the light. Those are the Fire's buddies, and they will stay there forever.

DUA 6.

RECITE ONCE IN THE MORNING

TRANSLITERATION

Bismillaahir Rahmaa-nir Raheem

Lillaahi maa fis-samaawaati wama fil ard;

Wa in'tubdoo ma-fee an'fusikum aw tukh-foohu yu'haa-sibkum bihil-laa;

Fa-yagh'firuli maiya-shaa'u wa-yu'adhibu maiya-shaa;

Wallahu ala kulee shay'in qadeer.

TRANSLATION

In the name of Allah, the Most Forgiving, the Most Merciful.

All that is in the heavens and all that is on earth belongs to Allah. Whether you reveal what is within of you or keep it hidden, Allah will hold you accountable for it. Then, as Allah is capable of all things, He will pardon or punish anybody He chooses.

DUA 7.

RECITE ONCE IN THE MORNING

TRANSLITERATION

Aa-manar rasulu bimaa un'zila ilaihi mir-Rabbihee wal-mu'minoon;

Kul'lun aa-mana billahi wamalaa-ikathi'hee wa-kutu-bhi'hee wa-rusu'lihee,

Laa-nufar'riqu baina ahadim mir-rusulih;

Wa-qaloo sami'naa wa-aata'naa;

Ghufra-naka rabbana wa-ilaikal maser.

TRANSLATION

Both the believers and the messenger have accepted what his lord revealed to them. They all professed faith in Allah, his angels, his revelations, and his messengers, declaring that we do not distinguish between any of his messengers. They respond, "we hear, and we obey." our lord, you are the [ultimate] goal, and [we want] your pardon.

DUA 8.

RECITE ONCE IN THE MORNING

TRANSLITERATION

Laa yukalliful-laahu nafsan illaa wus'ahaa;

Lahaa ma-kasabat wa-aa'laihaa mak-tasabat;

Rabbana laa tu'aakhid-naa in'naa-seenaa aw-akhtaa'naa;

Rabbana wa-laa tahmil-alainaa isran kamaa hamal'tahoo alal-ladhina min qablinaa;

Rabbana wala tu'ham-milna ma-laa-taa qata-lanaa bih;

Wa'fu ann'aa waghfir-lana war-ham'naa;

DR IBRAHIM SAYUTI

Anta mawlana fansur-na alal qaw-mil
kaa'fireen.

TRANSLATION

A soul can only be charged by Allah with
what it is capable of. It will experience the
[results] of the [good] it has attained and
[the results] of the [bad] it has attained.
Lord, forgive us if we have forgotten or made
a mistake. Our Lord, spare us the same load
You gave to those who came before us. Our
Lord, spare us the weight of anything we are
unable to bear. And forgive us, and have pity
on us, and pardon us. Give us success over
the skeptics; you are our protection.

9. SURAH AL IKHLAS

RECITE THREE TIMES IN THE MORNING

TRANSLITERATION

Bismillaahir Rahmaa-nir Raheem

1.Qul hu'wallaa-hu ahad.

2. Allah hus-samad.

3. Lam yalid wa-lam yoou'lad.

4. Wa-lam'ya kul-lahu kufu'wan ahad.

TRANSLATION

In the name of Allah, the Most Forgiving, the Most Merciful.

1. Declare that He is Allah, the One.

2. Allah is the Everlasting Refuge.

3. He neither bears children nor is born.

4 Nor is there any parallel to Him.

10.   SURAH AL FALAQ.

RECITE THREE TIMES IN THE MORNING

<u>TRANSLITERATION</u>

Bismillaahir Rahmaa-nir Raheem

1. **Qul a'udhubi rabbil falaq.**
2. **Min sharri ma khalaq.**
3. **Wa-min sharri gha'siqin idha waqab.**
4. **Wa-min shar'rin naf'faa thaati'fil uqad.**
5. **Wa-min shar'ri haa'sidin idha hasad.**

<u>TRANSLATION</u>

In the name of Allah, the Most Forgiving, the Most Merciful.

1. I take refuge in the Lord of dawn, you say.

2. From the wickedness He wrought in everything He made.
3. As well as when darkness descends, from its evil.
4. As well as from the blowers' wickedness in knots.
5. As well as from the bad an envier does when he envies.

11.   SURAH AN NAS.

RECITE THREE TIMES IN THE MORNING

TRANSLITERATION

Bismillaahir Rahmaa-nir Raheem

1 Qul a'udhubi rab'binn naas.

2 Malik'inn naas.

3 Ilaa hin'naas.

4 Min shar'ril was-wasil khan'naas.

5 Alladhee yu'was wi'su fee sudoo rin'naas.

6 Minal jin'nati wan naas.

DR IBRAHIM SAYUTI

TRANSLATION

In the name of Allah, the Most Forgiving, the Most Merciful.

1. I seek solace in the Lord of mankind, you shall say.
2. 2.The Humanity's Sovereign.
3. The Creator of humanity.
4. 4 From the whisperer's evil slinking away.
5. 5 Who whispers [evil] in people's hearts.
5 From both the Jinn and the human race.

12.   DUA FOR PROTECTION.

RECITE ONCE IN THE MORNING

Asbahna wa-asbahal mulku lillah;

Wal-hamdu lillah;

Laa-ilaaha illal-lah;

Wah-da'hu la-sharee kalah;

Lahul mulku wa-lahul hamd;

Yuh-yee wa-yu'meetu wa-huwa ala kulli shayin qadeer;

Rabbi ass-aaluka khay'ra mafee ha-dhal yaw'm;

Wa-khayra ma-ba'dah;

Wa-a'oodhu-bika min sharri'ma fee ha-dhal yaw'm;

Wa-sharri ma-ba'dah;

Rabbi a'oodhu-bika minal-kasali, wa-soo'il kibar;

Rabbi a'oodhu-bika min adha-bin fin'nari wa-adha-bin fil'qabr.

TRANSLATION

We have reached the morning and at this very time unto Allah belongs all sovereignty, and all praise is for Allah. None has the right to be worshipped except Allah, alone, without a partner, to Him belongs all sovereignty and praise and He is over all things omnipotent. My Lord, I ask You for the good of this day and the good of what follows it and I take refuge in You from the evil of this day and the evil of what follows it. My Lord, I take refuge in You from laziness and senility.

DUA 13
RECITE ONCE IN THE MORNING

TRANSLITRATION

Asbahna ala fitratil-islam;

Wa'ala kalimatil-ikhlas;

Wa'ala deeni nabi'yyina Muhammadin sallalla-hu alai'hi wasallam;

Wa'ala millati abeena Ibrahima hanee'fam muslimaa;

Wamaa kaana minal-mushrikeen.

TRANSLATION

We have risen the morning upon the fitrah of al-Islam, and the word of pure faith, and upon the religion of our Prophet Muhammad and the religion of our forefather Ibrahim, who was a Muslim and of the true faith and was not among those who equate others with Allah.

DUA 14
RECITE ONCE IN THE MORNING
DUA FOR SUBMISSIVE TO ALLAH

TRANSLITRATION

Allahumma bika asbahna;

Wa'bika amsaina;

Wa'bika nahya;

Wa'bika namoot;

Wa'ilay'kan nushoor.

TRANSLATION

By Your permission, O Allah, we have arrived at sunrise and evening, we live and die by Your permission, and our return is to You.

DUA 15
RECITE THREE TIMES IN THE MORING

TRANSLITERATION

Allahumma inni asbahtu minka fee-ni'matee'ou wa'aa fee-yatee'ou wa-sitr;

Fa aa'timma alay'ya ni'matak;

Wa-aa fee'yatak;

Wa-sit'raka fid-dunya wal-aakhira.

TRANSLATION

O Allah, I have awoken with Your blessings, your strength, and Your concealment of my faults; grant me the rest of Your blessings,

Your strength, and Your concealment in this life and the Hereafter.

DUA 16
RECITE ONCE IN THE MORING

TRANSLITERATION

Allahumma ma- asbaha bee'min nia'mah;

Aw'bi a'hadim min-khal'qik;

Fa-minka wah-dhaka laa-sharee kalak;

Fa-lakal hamdu wa-lakash shuk'r.

TRANSLATION

O Allah, every blessing that I or any member of Your creation have experienced is solely due to You; therefore, you alone deserve all praise and gratitude.

DUA 17
RECITE ONCE IN THE MORNING

DR IBRAHIM SAYUTI

TRANSLIRATION

Ya Rabbi lakal hamdu kama yam-baghi'li jalali waj-hika wa-adheemi sultanik.

TRANSLATION

All glory and honor, O my Lord, are Yours, as it benefits You might and the height of Your power.

DUA 18

RECITE THREE TIMES IN THE MORNING

DUA TO BE PLEASED

TRANSLITRATION

Radeetu billahi Rabba;

Wa'bil-islami dee'naa;

Wa-bi Muhammadin sal-lallahu alai'hi wa'sallama nabiy'yaw wa-rasulaa.

TRANSLATION

I acknowledge Muhammad as the Prophet and Messenger of Allah, and I have accepted Allah as my Lord and Islam as my way of life.

DUA 19
RECITE ONCE IN THE MORNING

DUA OF SALVATION

TRANSLITRATION

Allahumma innee as-aalukal af'wa wal-aa'fiyah;

Fid-dunya wal-akhirah;

Allahumma innee as'alukal a'fwa wal-aa'fiyah;

Fi-dee'nee wa-dunya'ya;

Wa-ahlee wama-lee;

Allah hummas-tur aw-raa'tee;

Wa-aa'mir raw-aa'tee;

Wah fadh-nee mim bai'nee ya-dai'yaa;

Wa-min khal-fee;

Wa-an ya'mee-nee;

Wa-an shee-malee,

Wa-min faw'qee;

Wa-a'udhubi adha-matika aan oogh-tala min tah'tee.

TRANSLATION

I pray to Allah for forgiveness and happiness in this life and the next. O Allah, I beg You for forgiveness and prosperity in my family, in the globe, and in my possessions. I seek refuge with You lest the earth swallows me up, O Allah, conceal my frailties, calm my fright, and protect me from the front and the back, on my right and my left, and from above.

DUA 20

THREE TIMES IN THE MORNING

TRANSLIRATION

SubhanAllahi wa-bihamdih;

Aa-dada khal'qih;

Wa-rida nafsih;

Wa-zinata a'rshih;

Wa-midada kalimatih.

TRANSLATION

How magnificent Allah is! I thank Him for His many creations, His joy, the size of His throne, and the ink on His writings.

DUA 21

RECITE THREE TIMES IN THE MORNING

TRANSLITERATION

Bismillah hil'ladhi la yadur'oo ma'as-mihi shai'un fil-ardi wa-laa fis'samaa;

Wa-hu'waas samee'ul alim.

TRANSLATION

DR IBRAHIM SAYUTI

In the name of Allah, who is the All-Hearing, the All-Knowing, and in whose name, nothing is damaged on earth or in the skies,

DUA 22

RECITE THREE TIMES IN THE MORNING

TRANLITRATION

Allahumma inni a'udhu-bika min an ush'rika bika shai'an aa'lam;

Wa-as'tagfiruka le-ma-la a'alam.

TRANSLATION

O Allah, I ask Your forgiveness for my unintentional actions and take refuge in You should I deliberately practice shirk with You.

DUA 23

PROTECTION AGAINST EVIL

RECITE THREE TIMES IN THE MORNING

TRANSLITRATION

A'oodhu-bi kalimaa-tillaah-hit taam'mati min sharri ma-khalaq.

TRANSLATION

In the beautiful words of Allah, I ask for protection from all the evil He has made.

DUA 24

RECITE ONCE IN THE MORNING

TRANSLITERATION

Allahumma aa'limal-ghaybi wash-shahadah;

Fati'ras samawati wal'ard;

Rabba kulli shay'in wama-leekah;

Ash'hadu al'laa ilaaha illa ant'h;

A'udhu-bika min shar'ri nafsee;

Wa'min shar'rish shay'taani wa-shirki;

Wa'an aq-tarifa ala-nafsee soo'an aw-a'joor-rahoo ila Muslim.

TRANSLATION

I vouch for the fact that only You are deserving of worship, O Allah, Knower of the Seen and the Unseen, Maker of the Heavens and the Earth, Lord, and Sustainer of All Things. I seek refuge in You for protection from the evil in my spirit, the evil and shirk of the devil, and from harming my soul or inflicting it on another Muslim.

DUA 25

RECITE ONCE IN THE MORNING

TRANSLATION

Ya hayyu ya qay'yuum;

Bi-rah'matika asta'geeth;

As-lih li-sha'ni kullah;

Wa-la takil'ni ila nafsee tarfata ayn.

TRANSLATION

O Ever Living, O Self-Sustained and Sustaining of All, I beseech Your Mercy; right for me all of my concerns; and do not leave me to my own devices, not even for a moment.

DUA 26

RECITE ONCE IN THE MORNING

DUA SAYYIDUL ISTIGHFAR

TRANSLITRATION

Allahumma anta rab'bee laa-ilaaha illa anta Khalaq-tanee;

Wa-ana ab'duk;

DR IBRAHIM SAYUTI

Wa-ana ala aah'dika wa-wa-dika mas'ta-taat;

A'udhu-bika min sharri ma-sanath;

Aboo'u laka bini'matika aalai'yaa;

Wa-aboo'u bi-tham'bee;

Fagh'fir lee;

Fa-inna'hu la-yagh'firu dhunooba illa ant.

TRANSLATION

Almighty Allah, you are my Lord; no one else has the right to receive worship save You; You created me, and I am Your servant; I do my best to uphold Your covenant and promise; and I seek refuge in You from the wrongdoing I have done. I recognize Your favor toward me and my sin; please pardon me, for only You can pardon sin.

DUA 27

RECITE FOUR TIMES IN THE MORNING

DUA OF AFIAT

TRANSLITERATION

Allahumma innee asbah'tu;

Ush-hiduka wa-ush'hidu hamalata ar'shik;

Wa-malaa ika'tak;

Wa-jamee'aa khalqik;

Ann'naka antal-lahu;

Laa-ilaaha illa ant;

Wah-daka laa-sharee kalak;

Wa-anna Muhammadan abdu'ka wa-rasooluk.

TRANSLATION

O Allah, in truth, I have arrived at dawn. I call upon You, Your throne bearers, Your angels, and the entirety of Your created beings to bear witness that You are Allah, that You alone have the right to be worshipped without a companion, and that Muhammad is Your servant and Messenger.

DUA 28
RECITE THREE TIMES IN THE MORNING

TRANSLIRATION

Allahumma aa'fi-nee fee bada'nee;

Allahumma aa'fi-nee fee sam'ee;

Allahumma aa'fi-nee fee basa'ree;

Laa-ilaaha illa ant;

Allahumma innee a'udhu-bika minal-kufri wal-faqr;

Wa-a'udhu-bika min adha-bil qabr;

Laa-ilaaha illa ant.

TRANSLATION

O Allah, please give me good health in all three of these areas: body, hearing, and sight. Only You, O Allah, have the right to be adored. Along with poverty and skepticism, I seek refuge with You from the wrath of the afterlife. Only you have the right to be worshipped.

DUA 29

DUA TO GET RIDE OF WORRIES

RECITE SEVEN TIMES IN THE MORNING

TRANSLITRATION

Hasbi-yallahu laa-ilaaha illa huwa aa'layhi tawak-kalth;

Wa-huwa rabbul ar'shil adheem.

TRANSLATION

I have enough faith in Allah to know that He alone is worthy of worship, and that He is also the Lord of the elevated throne.

DUA 30

RECITE ONCE IN THE MORNING

TRANSLITRATION

Asbahna wa-asbahal mulku lillahi, rabbil aa'la-meen;

Allahumma innee as-aluka khay'ra ha-dhal yaw'm;

Fath'hahoo wa nas'rahoo;Wa-noo'rahoo, wa baraka'tahoo, wa hudaah;Wa-a'oodhu-bika min shar-ri'ma feeh;   Wa-shar'ri ma ba'dah.

TRANSLATION

Now that morning has arrived, Allah, the Creator of the universe, is the sole king. O Allah, I ask You for this day's good, including its triumphs, victories, light, blessings, and guidance. I also seek refuge in You from this day's bad and the evil that will come after it.

DUA 31

RECITE 100 TIMES IN THE MORING

TRANSLITRATION

Laa-ilaaha illallahu wah dahu la-sharee kalah;

Lahul mulku wa-lahul hamd;

Wa-huwa ala kulee shay'in qadeer.

TRANSLATION

Only Allah has the right to be praised, alone and without a companion. He is the only one who is worthy of praise and has unlimited power over everything.

DUA 32

RECITE 100 TIMES IN THE MORNING

TRANSLITERATION

Subhanallahi wa-bi'hamdihi;

Subhanallah hil-adheem.

TRANSLATION

All acclaim and glory belong to Allah, who is also known as the Great.

DR IBRAHIM SAYUTI

CHAPTER TWO

EVENING AZKAR

RECITE ONCE IN THE EVENING

1. AL FATIHA (THE OPENING)
RECITE ONCE IN THE MORNING

TRANSLITERATION

5. **Bismillaahir Rahmaa-nir Raheem.**
6. **Alhamdu lillaahi rabbil aa'lameen.**
7. **Ar-rahmaa nir-raheem.**
8. **Maaliki'yaw mid-deen.**

7 . Iyyaa kana'budu wa-lyyaa kanasta'een.

8   Ih'dinas siraa'tal mustaqeem.

7. Siraatal-ladheena an'amta alai'him ghayril maghdoo bi'alai'him wa'lad daal-leen.

TRANSLATION

1. In the name of Allah, the Most Merciful, the Most Compassionate.

2. All praise is due to Allah, the creator of the universe.

3. The Forgiving and the Particularly Forgiving.

4. Ruler of the Day of Restitution.

5. We worship You and seek assistance from You.

6. Lead us along the right road.

7. The way of those You have shown favor to, not the way of those who have incited [Your] wrath or the way of the lost.

DR IBRAHIM SAYUTI

DUA 2

RECITE ONCE IN THE EVENING

TRANSLITERATION

Bismillaahir Rahmaanir Raheem

1 Alif Laam Meem.

2 Zaalikal kitaabu-laa raiba : feeh : hudal-lil muttaqeen.

3 Allazeena yu'minoona bilghaibi wa yu'qee-moonas salata wa mim'maa razaqna'hum yun'fiqoon.

4 Wal'lazena yu'minoona bimaa un'zila ilaika wa-maa unzila min qablika wa bil aa'khirati hum yu'qinoon.

5 Ulaa'ika aa'laa hudam-mir rabbihim; wa ulaa'ika humul muflihoon.

TRANSLATION

In the name of Allah, the Most Merciful, the Most Complete

1. Alif-Lam-Mim is One of the miracles of the Qur'an is these letters, and only Allah knows what they mean.
2. A manual for people who are awareof Allah, this book is the one about which there can be no question.
3. who establish prayer, have faith in the unseen, and give from what We have given them.
4. And those who have confidence in what has been revealed to you, [O Muhammad], what has been revealed before you, and what will be revealed in the Hereafter.
5. Those who have the appropriate direction from their Lord succeed.

DUA 3
RECITE ONCE IN THE EVENING

DR IBRAHIM SAYUTI

TRANSLITERATION

Bismillaahir Rahmaanir Raheem

Allahu laa ilaaha illaa'hu wal haiyul qai-yoom;

Laa taa'khuzuhoo sinatu'oo walaa na'woom;

Lahoo maa fis'samaawaati wa-maa fil ard;

Man, zal'lazee yashfa'oo in'dahoo illa be iznih;

Ya'lamu maa baina ai'deehim wa'maa khal-fahum;

Wa'laa yuhee'toona bee'shai-im'min il'mihee illa be-maa shaa;

Wasi'aa kursi'yuhus samaa-waati wal arda;

Wa'laa yaoo'duhoo hif'zuhumaa wa huwal ali'yyul azeem.

TRANSLATION

In the name of Allah, the Most Merciful, the Most Complete

Only Allah, the Ever-Living, the Sustainer of Existence, exists as a deity. He is not overpowered by sleep or lethargy. Both the sky and the earth are His, and they both

belong to Him. Who among us has the power to petition Him without His consent? They do not include anything from His knowledge other than what He wills, even though He knows what is [now] before them and what will come after them. His Kursi encompasses both the sky and the earth, and He is unfazed by the maintenance of either. Additionally, He is Most High and Most Great.

DUA 4

RECITE ONCE IN THE EVENING

TRANSLITERATION

Laa ik'raaha fid-deen;

Qat-tabiya'nar rushdu minal ghayy;

Famai 'yakfur bit taa'ghooti wa yu'mim billaahi faqadis tamsaka bil'urwatil wusqaa lan-fisaama lahaa;

Wallaahu samee'un aleem.

TRANSLATION

The acceptance of the religion shall not be forced. The right path has become more obvious than the incorrect one. Whoever rejects Taught and adheres to the teachings of Allah has so firmly grasped the most solid handhold. Allah also hears and knows.

DUA 5
RECITE ONCE IN THE EVENING

TRANSLITERATION

Allaahu waliyyul lazeena aa'manoo yukh'rijuhum minaz-zulumaati ilan noor;

Wal'lazee na-kafaroo awliyaa uo'humut taa'ghootu yukh'rijoo-nahum minan noori ilaz-zulumaat;

Ulaa'ika as'haabun naari hum fee'haa khaa'lidoon.

TRANSLATION

Allah is the ally of those who believe. He brings them out of the darkness into the light. And those who disbelieve—their allies are Taught. They take them out of the light and into darkness. Those are the companions of the fire; they will abide eternally therein.

DUA 6
RECITE ONCE IN THE EVENING

TRANSLITERATION

Bismillaahir Rahmaanir Raheem

Lillaahi maa fis-samaawaati wa-maa fil ard;

Wa in'tubdoo maa feee an'fusikum aw tukh-foohu yuhaa-sibkum bihil-laa;

Fayagh'firuli maiya-shaa'u wa yu'azzibu maiya-shaa;

Wallaahu aa'laa kulli shai in qadeer.

TRANSLATION

In the name of Allah, the Most Merciful, the Most Complete

DR IBRAHIM SAYUTI

Everything on earth and in the skies belongs to Allah. Whether you reveal what is within of you or keep it hidden, Allah will hold you accountable for it. Allah is capable of handling anything, thus He will pardon or punish anybody He chooses.

DUA 7
RECITE ONCE IN EVENING

TRANSLITERATION

Aa'manar-rasoolu bimaa un'zila ilaihi mir-Rabbihee walmu'minoon;

Kul'lun aa'mana billaahi wa malaa'ikathihee wa kutubhihee wa rusulihee,

Laa nufar'riqu baina ahadim-mir-rusulih;

Wa qaaloo sami'naa wa aata'naa;

Ghufra-naka rabbana wa ilaikal maser.

TRANSLATION

Both the believers and the Messenger had accepted what his Lord revealed to them.

54

They all claimed to believe in Allah, His angels, His writings, and His messengers, declaring that they did not distinguish between any of them. They respond, "We hear, and we obey." Our Lord, you are the [ultimate] goal, and [we want] Your pardon.

DUA 8
RECITE ONCE IN EVENING

TRANSLITERATION

Laa yukalliful-laahu nafsan illaa wus'ahaa;

Lahaa maa kasabat wa aa'laihaa mak-tasabat;

Rabbana laa tu'aakhiznaa in'naa-seenaa aw-akhtaa'naa;

Rabbana wa laa tahmil-alainaa isran kamaa hamaltahoo alal-lazeena min qablinaa;

Rabbana wa laa tuham-milnaa maa laa taa'qata lanaa bih;

Wa'fu annaa waghfir lanaa war'hamnaa;

Anta mawlana fansur-naa alal qawmil kaafireen.

TRANSLATION

A soul can only be charged by Allah with what it can handle. It will experience the effects of any good it has attained as well as the effects of any evil. Lord, forgive us if we have forgotten or made a mistake. Please, Lord, spare us the same load You gave to those who came before us. Please, Lord, do not put anything upon us that we are unable to endure. And please have compassion on us, forgive us, and pardon us. Give us success over the skeptics; you are our protection.

DUA 9
RECITE THREE TIMES IN THE EVENING

TRANSLITERATION

Bismillaahir Rahmaanir Raheem

1. Qul hu'wallaa-hu ahad.

2. Allah hus-samad.
3. Lam yalid wa-lam yoou'lad.
4. Wa lam'ya kul-lahu kufu'wan ahad.

TRANSLATION

In the name of Allah, the Most Merciful, the Most Complete

1. Declare that He is Allah, the One.
2. Allah is the Everlasting Refuge;
3. He never gives birth nor is given.
4. Furthermore, He has no counterpart.

DUA 10

RECITE THREE TIMES IN THE EVENING

TRANSLITERATION

Bismillaahir Rahmaanir Raheem

1. Qul a'uzoo-bi rabbil-falaq.
2. Min sharri ma khalaq.
3. Wa min sharri gha'siqin iza waqab.
4. Wa min shar'rin naf'faa saati'fil uqad.
5. Wa min shar'ri haa'sidin iza hasad.

TRANSLATION

In the name of Allah, the Most Merciful, the Most Complete

1. I seek solace in the Lord of dawn, you say.
2. from the bad He wrought in what He created.
3. from the darkness's evil as it comes to rest.
4. and from the blowers' wickedness in knots.
5. And from the bad an envious person does when he envies.

DUA 11
RECITE THREE TIMES IN THE EVENING

58

TRANSLITERATION

Bismillaahir Rahmaanir Raheem

1. Qul a'uzu-bi rab'binn naas.
2. Malik'inn naas.
3. Ilaa hin'naas.
4. Min shar'ril waas-wa-asil khan'naas.
5. Al lazee yu'was wi'su fee sudoo-rin naas.
6. Minal jin'nati wan naas.

TRANSLATION

In the name of Allah, the Most Merciful, the Most Complete

1. I seek refuge in the Lord of mankind, you say.
2. He is the ruler of all people.
3. The God of Humanity,
4. from the whisperer's poisonous retreat.
5. Who whispers [evil] in humankind's breasts?
6. From among the jinn and people,

DR IBRAHIM SAYUTI

DUA 12
RECITE ONCE IN THE EVENING

TRANSLITERATION

Amsaina wa-amsal mulku lillah;

Wal-hamdu lillah;

La ilaha illal-lah;

Wah-da'hoo la-sharee kalah;

Lahul-mulku wa'lahul-hamd;

Yuh-ee wa yu'meeto wa'huwa ala kulli shayin qadeer;

Rabbi ass-aaluka khay'ra mafee haa-zee'hil lai'lah;

Wa-khayra ma ba'daha;

Wa- aa'ozu-bika min sharri ma fee haa-zee'hil lai'lah;

Wa sharri ma ba'daha;

Rabbi aa'ozu-bika minal-kasali, wa-soo-il kibar;

Rabbi aa'ozubika min aa'zaa-bin fin'nari wa aa'zaa-bin fil'qabr.

TRANSLATION

We have arrived at twilight, and at this very moment, Allah alone possesses full dominion. Only Allah has the right to be praised, alone and without a companion. He is the only one who is worthy of praise and has unlimited power over everything. My Lord, I beseech You for the good of this night and the good that will come after it, and I seek refuge in You from the bad that will come with both of those things. I seek refuge in you, O Lord, from senility and sloth. I seek refuge in you, O Lord, from the fire's pain and the grave's retribution.

DUA 13
RECITE ONCE IN THE EVENING

TRANSLITERATION

Aamsaina ala fitratil-islam;

Wa'ala kalimatil-ikhlas;

DR IBRAHIM SAYUTI

Wa'ala deeni nabi'yyina Muhammadin sallalla-hu alai'hi wasallam;

Wa'ala millati abeena Ibrahima hanee'faan muslimah;

Waama kana minal-mushrikeen.

TRANSLATION

We have made it at dusk based on the fitrah of Al-Islam, the message of unadulterated faith, and the religions of our Prophet Muhammad and Ibrahim, who was a Muslim and a person of real faith who did not belong to those who identify other people with Allah.

DUA 14
RECITE ONCE IN THE EVENING

TRANSLITERATION

Allahumma bika amsaina;

Wa'bika asbahna;

Wa'bika nahya;

Wa'bika namooth;

Wa'ilay'kaal maser.

TRANSLATION

By Your permission, O Allah, we have arrived at both the nighttime and the morning. We are given life and death, and our return is to You.

DUA 15

RECITE THREE TIMES IN THE EVENING

TRANSLITERATION

Allahumma inni aam'saitu minka fee-ni'matee'ou wa'aa fee-yatee'ou wa sitr;

Fa aa'timma alayya ni'matak;

Wa'aa fee'yatak;

Wa sit'raka fid-dunya wal akhira

DR IBRAHIM SAYUTI

TRANSLATION

I've made it till the evening, O Allah, thanks to Your blessings, Your strength, and Your hiding of my flaws. So please provide me all of Your blessings, all of Your power, all of Your secrecy for both this life and the next.

DUA 16
RECITE ONCE IN THE EVENING

TRANSLITERATION

Allahumma ma aamsa bee'min nia'mah;

Aw'bee a'haa-deem min khal'qik;

Fa'minka wah-dhaka la-sharee kalak;

Fa-lakal hamdu wa-lakash shukr.

TRANSLATION

O Allah, whatever blessings that I or any of Your creation have received are all due to

You; therefore, you alone deserve all praise and gratitude.

DUA 17

RECITE ONCE IN THE EVENING

TRANSLITERATION

Ya Rabbi lakal hamdu kama yam-baghi'li jalali waj'hika wa'azimi sultanik.

TRANSLATION

All glory and honor, O my Lord, are Yours, as it befits You might and the height of Your power.

DUA 18

RECITE THREE TIMES IN THE EVENING

TRANSLITERATION

Radeetu billahi Rabbah;

DR IBRAHIM SAYUTI

Wa'bil-islami dee'nah;

Wa'bee Muhammadin sal-lallahu alai'hi wa'sallama nabiy'ya wa rasulaah.

TRANSLATION

I acknowledge Muhammad as the Prophet and Messenger of Allah, and I have accepted Allah as my Lord and Islam as my way of life.

DUA 19
RECITE ONCE IN THE EVENEING

TRANSLITERATION

Allahumma innee as-aalukal aaf'wa wal-aa'fiyah;

Fid-dunya wal-akhirah;

Allahumma innee as'alukal aa'fwa wal-aa'fiyah;

Fee dee'nee wa'dunya-ya;

Wa'ahlee wama-lee;

Allah hummas-tur aaw-ra'tee;

Wa aa'mir raw-aa'tee;

Wah fiz'nee min bai'nee ya-dai'yaa;

Wa-min khal'fee;

Wa'aai ya'mee-nee;

Wa'aai shee'malee,

Wa-min faw'qee;

Wa'aa-oozubi aa'zaa-matika aan oogh-tala min tahtee.

TRANSLATION

I pray to Allah for forgiveness and happiness in this life and the next. O Allah, I beg You for forgiveness and prosperity in my family, in the globe, and in my possessions. I seek refuge with You lest the earth swallows me up, O Allah, conceal my frailties, calm my fright, and protect me from the front and the back, on my right and my left, and from above.

DUA 20
RECITE THREE TIMES IN THE EVENING

TRANSLITERATION

SubhanAllahi wa-bihamdih;

Aa'dada khal'qi;

Wa'rida nafsih;

Wa'zinata aa'rshih;

Wa'midada kalimatih.

TRANSLATION

How magnificent Allah is! I thank Him for His many creations, His joy, the size of His throne, and the ink on His writings.

DUA 21
RECITE THREE TIMES IN THE EVENING

TRANSLITERATION

Bismillah hil'lazee la yadur'oo ma'aas-mihi shai-oon fil-ardi wa'laa fis-samaa;

Wa'hu'waas samee'ool aa'leem.

TRANSLATION

In the name of Allah, who is the All-Seeing, the All-Knowing, and in whose name, nothing is hurt on earth or in the sky.

DUA 22

RECITE THREE TIMES IN THE EVENING

TRANSLITERATION

Allahumma inni a'oozu-bika min aan ush'rika bika shai'an aa'lam;

Wa aas'tagfiruka le ma la a'alam.

TRANSLATION

O Allah, I ask Your forgiveness for my unintentional actions and take refuge in You should I deliberately practice shirk with You.

DUA 23
RECITE THREE TIMES IN THE EVENING

TRANSLITERATION

Aa'oozu-bi kalima-tillah heet-taam'mati min sharri ma khalaq.

TRANSLATION

In the beautiful words of Allah, I ask for protection from all the evil He has made.

DUA 24
RECITE ONCE IN THE EVENING

TRANSLITERATION

Allahumma aa'limal-ghaybi wash-shahadah;

Fati'ras samawati wal'ard;

Rabba kulli shay'in wa'ma leekah;

Ash'hadu al'laa ilaha illa anth;

Aa'ozu-bika min shar'ri nafsee;

Wa'min shar'rish shay'tani wa-shirki;

Wa'an aq-tarifa ala nafsee soo'an aw aa'joor-rahoo ila Muslim.

TRANSLATION

I testify to the fact that only You are deserving of worship, O Allah, Knower of the Seen and the Unseen, Maker of the Heavens and the Earth, Lord, and Sustainer of All Things. I seek refuge in You for protection from the evil in my spirit, the evil and shirk of the devil, and from harming my soul or inflicting it on another Muslim.

DUA 25
RECITE ONCE IN THE EVENING

TRANSLITERATION

DR IBRAHIM SAYUTI

Ya hayyu ya qay'yum;

Bi-rah'matika asta'gis;

As'lih li sha'ni kullah;

Wa'la takil'ni ila nafsi tarfata ayn.

TRANSLATION

O Ever Living, O Self-Sustained and Sustaining of All, I beseech Your Mercy; right for me all of my concerns; and do not leave me to my own devices, not even for a moment.

DUA 26
RECITE ONCE IN THE EVENING

TRANSLITERATION

Allahumma anta rab'bee la ilaha illa anta Khalaq-tanee;

Wa'ana aab'duk;

Wa'ana ala aah'dika wa-wa'dika mas'ta-taat;

Aa'ozu-bika min sharri ma'sanath;

Aa'boo'u laka bini'matika aalai'yaa;

Wa'aboo'u bi-zan'bee;

Fagh'fir lee;

Fa-inna'hu la yagh'firuz zunu'ba illa ant.

TRANSLATION

O Allah, you are my Lord; only You are worthy of worship; I am Your servant because You created me; I do my best to uphold Your covenant and promise; and I seek refuge in You from the wrongdoing I have done. I recognize Your favor toward me and my sin; please pardon me, for only You can pardon sin.

DUA 27
RECITE FOUR TIMES IN THE EVENING

TRANSLITERATION

Allahumma innee aam'sait;

Osh'hiduka wa-oshhidu hamalata aar'shik;

Wa'malaa ika'tak;

Wa-jamee'aa khalqik;

Ann'naka antal-lahu;

La ilaha illa ant;

Wah'daka laa sharee kalak;

Wa'anna Muhammadan aabdu'ka wa'rasooluk.

TRANSLATION

O Allah, in truth, it is now twilight, and I call upon You, your throne-bearers, Your angels, and the entirety of Your created beings to bear witness that You are Allah, that You alone have the right to be worshiped without a companion, and that Muhammad is Your servant and Messenger.

DUA 28
RECITE THREE TIMES IN THE EVENING

TRANSLITERATION

Allahumma aa'fi-nee fee bada'nee;

Allahumma aa'fi-nee fee sam'ee;

Allahumma aa'fi-nee fee basa'ree;

La ilaha illa-ant;

Allahumma innee aa'oozu-bika minal-kufri wal-faqr;

Wa'aa'oo-zu-bika min aa'zaa-bil-qabr;

La ilaha illa-ant.

TRANSLATION

O Allah, please give me good health in all three of these areas: body, hearing, and sight. Only You, O Allah, have the right to be adored. Along with poverty and skepticism, I seek refuge with You from the wrath of the afterlife. Only you have the right to be worshipped.

DUA 29
RECITE SEVEN TIMES IN THE EVENING

DR IBRAHIM SAYUTI

TRANSLITERATION

Hasbi-yallahu la ilaha illa huwa aa'layhi tawak-kalth;

Wa'huwa rabbul aar'shil aa'zeem.

TRANSLATION

I am blessed with sufficient faith in Allah to know that He alone is worthy of worship and that He is also the Lord of the elevated throne.

DUA 30

RECITE 100 TIMES IN THE EVENING

TRANSLITERATION

Laa ilaaha illallaahu wahdahu laa sha'ree kalah;

Lahul-mulku wa lahul-hamd;

Wa'huwa aa'laa kulli shay'in qadeer.

TRANSLATION

Only Allah has the right to be praised, alone and without a companion. He is the only one who is worthy of praise and has unlimited power over everything.

DUA 31

RECITE 100 TIMES IN THE EVENING

TRANSLITERATION

SubhanAllahi wa bi'hamdihi;

SubhanAllah-hil aa'zim

TRANSLATION

All appreciation and glory belong to Allah, who is also known as the Great.

CHAPTER 3

DUA AFTER SALAT

Verse 1 Dua

Bismillaahirrahmaanirrahiim.
Alhamdulillaahi rabbil 'aalamiin. Hamdan
yu-waafii ni'amahuuwayukaafi'u maziidah.
Yaa rabbanaa lakalhamdu wa lakasy syukru
kamaa yambaghii lijalaaliwajhika wa
'azhiimisul-thaanik.

TRANSLATION

All praise is given to Allah, Creator of the
Worlds—the Generous, the Merciful. Glory
be to His grace and greater reward. Praise be
to you, O our Lord, as you should be to the
grandeur, the kind face, and the awesome
power.

Comment [S]:

78

Allaahumma shalliwasallim 'ala sayyidinaa muhammadiw wa 'ala aali sayyidinaa muhammad shalaatan tun jihnaa bihatsa min jamii'il ahwaali wal aafaat. Wa taqdhii lanaa bihaa jamii'al hajaat. Wa tuthahhirunaa bihaa min jamits sayyi'aat. Wa tarfa 'unaabihaa 'indaka a'lad darajaat. Wa tuballighunaa bihaa aqshal gha yaati minjamii'il khairaati fil hayaati wa ba'dal mamaat. Innahu samii'un qariibum mujiibud da'awaat wayaa qaadhiyal hajaat

TRANSLATION

O Allah, grant our Prophet Muhammad and his family grace and wealth, for it is a grace that can deliver us from all dread and disease, satisfy all our requirements, purify us from every sin, and elevate our station. to the fullest extent by Your side, and can lead us to the pinnacle of all virtue, both while we are alive and after we pass away. Allah is truly All-Hearing All-Near and All-Permitting of all requests and prayers. all that His servant requires.

Allaahumma innaa nas'aluka salaamatan fiddiini waddun-yaa wal aakhirah. Wa 'aafiyatun fil jasadi wa shillihatun fil badani wa ziyaadatan fil'ilmi wa barakatan firrizqi wa taubatan qablal maut wa rahmatan 'indalmaut wa maghfiratan ba'dal maut. Allaahumma hawwin 'alainaa fii sakaraatil maut wan najaata minannaari wal 'afwa 'indal hisaab.

TRANSLATION

O Allah, we want your protection in the realms of religion, the material world, and the Hereafter; wellbeing and health in the physical body; advancement in science; and blessings in this life. And pardon after death, mercy before death, and repentance. O Allah, spare us from the pain of death and the flames and grant us forgiveness for our transgressions.

Allaahumma innaa na 'uudzubika minal'ajzi wal kasali wal bukhli wal harami wa 'adzaabil qabri

Translation:

Dear Allah! genuinely, we seek refuge in You from frailty, sloth, frugalness, senility, and severe retribution.

Allahummaa innaa na'uudzubika min'ilmin laa yanfa'u wa min qalbii laa yakhsya'u wa min nafsin laa tasyaba'u wa min da'watin laa yustajaabu lahaa

TRANSLATION

Dear Allah! We seek refuge in you from irrational knowledge, an unfaithful heart, an unsatisfied soul, and an unfulfilled dua.

Rabbanagh firlanaa dzunuubanaa wa liwaalidiinaa walimasyaayikhinaa wa limu'alli-miinaa wa liman lahuu haqqun 'alainaa wa liman ahabba wa ahsana ilainaa wa likaaffatil mus limiin ajma'iin

TRANSLATION

DR IBRAHIM SAYUTI

O Our Lord, forgive our sins, the sins of our parents, our elders, our instructors, those who have authority over us, those who love and benefit from us, and the sins of all Muslims," is the correct

Rabbanaa taqabbal minnaa innaka antas samii'ul 'aliim, wa tub'alainaa innaka antat tawwabur rahiim

TRANSLATION:

Oh, our Lord, grant our request; You are all-hearing and all-knowing, so please do. Accept our contrition, for You are Most Merciful and Accepting of Repentance.

Rabbanaa aatinaa fiduunnyaa hasanah, wa fil aakhirati hasanah, waqinaa 'adzaa ban naar

TRASNLATION

"Our Lord, preserve us from the torture of the fire and grant us goodness in this life and the hereafter."

Washallallahu 'alaa sayyidinaa muhammadin wa'alaa aalihiwa shahbihiiwa sallam, wal hamdu lillaahirabbil 'aalamiin

TRANSLATION

All glory be to Allah, Lord of the Universe, and may Allah grant kindness and prosperity to our Prophet Muhammad, his family, and the sahabah."

Bismillahirrahmaanirrahiim. Alhamdu Lillaahi Rabbil 'aalamiin, Hamdan Yuwaafii Ni'amahu Wayukaafii Maziidah. Ya Rabbanaa Lakal Hamdu Kamaa Yam Baghhi Lijalaali Wajhikal Kariimi Wa'azhiimi Sulthaanik."

TRANSLATION

"In the name of Allah, the merciful, the beneficial." Praise be to Allah, the Creator of the Worlds. Glory be to His grace and greater reward. Praise be to you, O our Lord,

DR IBRAHIM SAYUTI

as it is fitting for your grandeur, kind face, and immense power.

Allahumma Shalli 'alaa Sayyidinaa Muhammadi Wa'alaa Aali Sayyidinaa Muhammad".

TRANSLATION

O Allah, grant our Prophet Muhammad and his family grace and prosperity."

"Allahumma Rabbanaa Taqabbal Minnaa Shalaataana Washiyaamanaa Warukuu'anaa Wasujuudanaa Waqu'uudanaa Watadlarru'anaa, Watakhasysyu'anaa Wata'abbudanaa, Watammim Taqshiiranaa Yaa Allah Yaa Rabbal'aalamiin".

TRANSLATION

O Allah, please accept our prayers, our fast, our bow, our prostrations, our sitting, our humility, our devotion, and complete what we do during our prayers, O Allah, Lord of the whole world."

"Rabbana Dzholamnaa Anfusanaa Wa-inlamtaghfir Lana Watarhamnaa Lanakuunanna Mlnal Khaasiriin".

TRANSLATION

Our Lord, we have mistreated ourselves, and we will undoubtedly be among the losers if You do not forgive us and have compassion upon us," the Qur'an says.

"Rabbanaa Walaa Tahmil'alainaa Ishran Kama Hamaltahul'alal Ladziina Min Qablinaa. "

"Our Lord, do not place upon us a burden like that which You placed upon those before us," the translation reads.

Rabbanaa Walaa Tuhammilnaa Maalaa Thaaqata Lanaa Bihii Wa'fu'annaa Waghfir Lanaa Warhamnaa Anta Maulaanaa Fanshurnaa 'alal Qaumil Kaafiriin".

DR IBRAHIM SAYUTI

Please, Lord, do not subject us to something that we are unable to bear. And please have compassion on us, forgive us, and pardon us. As our guardian, please grant us victory over the skeptics.

"Rabbanaa Laa Tuzigh Quluubanaa Ba'da Idzhadaitanaa W'ahablanaa Min Ladunka Rahmatan Innaka Antal Wahhaab".

"Our Lord, do not let our souls wander after You have led us and shown us mercy from Yourself," the translation reads. You are the giver.

"Rabbanaghfir Lanaa Waliwaalidinaa Walijami'il Muslimiin Walmuslimaati Wal Mu'miniina Walmu'minati. Al Ahyaa-i-minhum Wal Amwaati, Innaka Alaa Kuli Syai'n Qadiir".

TRANSLATION

O Allah, forgive our sins and the sins of our parents, and for all Muslim men and women, male and female believers, whether living or dead. Verily Allah has power over all things"

DUA TO SEEK REFUGE FROM PUNISHMENT ON THE JUDGEMENT DAY

"Robbi Qinii 'Adzaabaka Yauma Tab'atsu'Ibaadaka."

"O Allah, shield me from Your retribution on the day when Your servants are raised to life," is the literal translation.

CHAPTER 4

DHIKR AFTER SALAH

ISTIGHFAR

"Astaghfirul-lah, astaghfirullah, astaghfirullah, allahumma antassalam

waminkassalam tabarakta ya dzaljalali wal
ikram"

TRANSLATION

**I beg Allah's pardon. (Twice) "O Allah, you
are As-Salam, and there is no other source of
peace except You; blessed are You, O
Possessor of Majesty and Honor." The One
Who is without flaws and shortcomings (AS-
Salam).**

TAUHID

laa ilaaha illallahu wahdahu laa syarikalahu,
lahul mulku walahul hamdu wahuwa 'alaa
kulli syai-inq qodir, allahumma laa mani 'aa
lima a' thoita wala mughthiya lima
managhta wala yanfa'u dzaljaddi minkal
jaddu"

TRANSLATON

**No one has the right to be worshiped save
Allah, alone, without associate; all honor**

and dominion are due to Him, and He is the supreme power over all." No one can prevent what You have decided to bestow, and no one can grant what You have decided to prevent, O Allah. No one can gain from wealth or majesty because they all come from You.

laa ilaaha illallahu wahdahu laa syarikalahu, lahul mulku walahul hamdu wahuwa 'alaa kulli syai-inq qodir, laa haula wala quwwata illa billah, laa ilaaha illallahu wala na'budhu illa iyyahu, lahun ni'matu walahul fadhlu walahus sana'ul hasan, laa ilaaha illallahu mukhlisina lahuddin walau karihal khafirun"

TRANSLATION

No one has the right to be worshiped save Allah, alone, without associate; all honor and dominion are due to Him, and He is the supreme power over all." No one has the right to be worshiped other than Allah, and we are the only ones who are allowed to worship anyone else. All favor, all grace, and all heavenly adoration are for Him. Only Allah has the right to be worshipped, and even if the unbelievers abhor it, we are sincere in our faith and devotion to Him.

TASBIH, TAHMID AND TAKBIR

33x Subhanallah

Translation: How perfect Allah is

33x Alhamdulillah

Translation: All praise is for Allah.

Allahuakbar 33x

Translation: Allah is the greatest."(33x)

CONTINUE BY READING

"laa ilaaha illallahu wahdahu laa syarikalahu, lahul mulku walahul hamdu wahuwa 'alaa kulli syai-inq qodir"

Translation: "None has the right to be worshipped except Allah, alone, without a partner, to Him belongs all sovereignty and praise and He is over all things omnipotent

Ayatul Kursi ´

"allahu laa ilaaha illa huwal hayyul qayyumu. laa ta'khudzuhuu sinatuw wa laa nauum. lahuu maa fissamaawaati wa maa fil ardhi. man dzal ladzii yasfa'u'indahuu illaa bi idznihi. ya'lamu maa baina aidiihim wa maa khalfahum. wa laa yuhithuuna bi syai-in min 'ilmihii illaa bi maasyaa-a. wasi'a kursiyyuhussamaawaati wal ardha. wa laa ya-udhuu hifzhuhumaa wahuwal 'aliyyul azhiim."

TRANSLATION

"Allah! Other than He, the alive, the eternal, there is no other god. He isn't overtaken by sleep or slumber. Both the sky and the earth are His, and they both belong to Him. Who is the one who can appeal to Him without His consent? They are unable to understand any of His knowledge unless it is according to His desire. He knows what is ahead of them and what is behind them. The maintenance of both the heavens and the earth does not weigh on His throne. He is the Great and Most High.

Al-Baqarah: 255 (QS). Reference: "Death will be the only thing standing between whoever recites Aytul Kursi immediately after each obligatory Salah and entering Paradise."

SURAH AL-IKHLAS, AL-FALAQ & AN-NAS

The following three Soorahs should be recited once after Zuhr, 'Asr, and 'Ishaa Salah and thrice after the Fajr and Maghrib Salah.

SURAH AL-IKHLAS

Bismillahirrahmanirrahim,

1. Qul huwa allaahu ahad(un),
2. allaahu alshshamad(u),
3. lam yalid walam yuulad(u),
4. walam yakullahu kufuwan ahad(un).

TRANSLATION

In the name of Allah, the Most Merciful, the Most Complete

1. Declare that He is Allah, the One.
2. Allah is the Everlasting Refuge;
3. He never gives birth nor is given.
4. Furthermore, He has no counterpart.

SURAH AL-FALAQ

Bismillaahir Rahmaanir Raheem

1. Qul a'uzoo-bi rabbil-falaq.
2. Min sharri ma khalaq.
3. Wa min sharri gha'siqin iza waqab.
4. Wa min shar'rin naf'faa saati'fil uqad.
5. Wa min shar'ri haa'sidin iza hasad.

TRANSLATION

In the name of Allah, the Most Merciful, the Most Complete

1. I Seek Solace in The Lord of Dawn, You Say.

2. From The Bad He Wrought in What He Created.
3. From The Darkness's Evil as It Comes to Rest.
4. And From the Blowers' Wickedness In Knots.
5. And From the Bad an Envious Person Does When He Envies.

TRANSLITERATION

Bismillaahir Rahmaanir Raheem

1 Qul a'uzu-bi rab'binn naas.

2 Malik'inn naas.

3 Ilaa hin'naas.

5 Min shar'ril waas-wa-asil khan'naas.

6 Al lazee yu'was wi'su fee sudoo-rin naas.

7 Minal jin'nati wan naas.

TRANSLATION

In the name of Allah, the Most Merciful, the Most Complete

1. I seek refuge in the Lord of mankind, you say.
2. He is the ruler of all people.
3. The God of Humanity,
4. from the whisperer's poisonous retreat.
5. Who whispers [evil] in humankind's breasts?
6. From among the jinn and people,

GUIDE FOR SALAH

TAKBIRATUL IHRAM

Raise your hands to your ears and say:

Allahu Akbar Translation: "Allah is the Greatest

AL FATIHAH

1. Bismillaahir rahmaa-nir raheem.
2. Alhamdu lillaahi rabbil aa'lameen.
3. Ar-rahmaa-nir-raheem.
4. Maaliki yawmid-deen.
5. Iyyaaka na'budu wa Iyyaaka nasta'een.
6. Ihdinas siraa'tal mustaqeem.

7. Siraatal-lazeena an'amta 'alaihim ghayril maghdoo bi'alai'lilm wa lad-daalleen.

TRANSLATION

1. In The Name of Allah, The Most Gracious, The Most Gracious.
2. All Glory Belongs to Allah, The Creator of The Universe.
3. The Completely Merciful and The Particularly Merciful:
4. Ruler Of the Day of Restitution
5. We Worship You, And We Beg Your Assistance.
6. Show Us the Way to The Right Road.
7. The Way of Those You Have Shown Favor To, Not of Those Who Have Angered You or Who Are Misguided.

GUIDE FOR SALAH

RUKU'

(Bow down)

As you are bowing down say 'Allahu Akbar'. Make sure to keep your back straight, your hands on your knees, and your eyes focused on the ground where you will be prostrating. When you are in this position you will say this sentence three times:

SUBHANNA RABBEEYAL ADHEEM (3x)

Translation: "How perfect is my Lord, the Magnificent"

I'TIDAL (RISE FROM BOWING)

As you are rising from the ruku position to a standing position you will bring your hands to your ears and will say: SAMEE ALLAHU LEEMAN HAMEEDA

TRANSLATION: Allah hears those who praise him and when you are standing upright then lower your hands to your waist and say:

RABBANA WALAKAL HAMD

Translation: Our Lord, to You, is all praise

SUJUD (PROSTRATION)

kneel to do prostrations. Sujud is the name for this.

Say "Allahu akbar" as you get into this position.

Ensure that the palms of your hands, the backs of your knees, and the soles of your feet are all contacting the ground.

SUBHANNA RABBEEYAL 'ALAA 3 TIMES

Meaning How flawless is my God? He is the highest being.

RISE FROM SUJUD

Sit for a while after rising from sujud. After rising from sujud, sit on your left leg and recite Allahu akbar. While your right foot is standing upright, your left foot will be flat on the ground. Hands-on knees position. It is advised to seek Allah's pardon when you find yourself in this situation.

Here is a short and easy dua to recite:
RABBIGH- FIR LEE

MEANING: Our Lord Forgives Me

TASYAHUD AWAL

Attahiyyaatul mubaarokaatush sholawaatuth thoyyibaatu lillaah. Assalaamu 'alaika ayyuhan nabiyyu wa rohmatulloohi wa barokaatuh. Assalaaamu'alainaa wa 'alaa 'ibaadillaahish shoolihiin. Asyhadu allaa ilaaha illallooh wa asyhadu anna Muhammadar rosuulullooh. Allahummasholli ala Sayyidina Muhammad.

TASYAHUD AKHIR

Attahiyyaatul mubaarokaatush sholawaatuth thoyyibaatu lillaah. Assalaamu 'alaika ayyuhan nabiyyu wa rohmatulloohi wa barokaatuh. Assalaaamu'alainaa wa 'alaa 'ibaadillaahish shoolihiin. Asyhadu allaa ilaaha illallooh wa asyhadu anna

DR IBRAHIM SAYUTI

Muhammadar rosuululooh. Allahumma Shalli Ala Sayyidina Muhammad Wa Ala Ali Sayyidina Muhammad. Kama Shollaita Ala Sayyidina Ibrahim wa alaa aali sayyidina Ibrahim, wabaarik ala Sayyidina Muhammad Wa Alaa Ali Sayyidina Muhammad, Kama barokta alaa Sayyidina Ibrahim wa alaa ali Sayyidina Ibrahim, Fil aalamiina innaka hamiidummajid.

THE TASLEEM

After reciting the second part of the tashahud, you will say the tasleem.

The tasleem is to look to your right and say:

Assalamu alaykum wa rahmatu allah

 translation: peace and blessing from allah be upon you and then look to the left and say it again assalamu alaykum wa rahmatu allah

Translation: peace and belssingg from allah be upon you

DUA QUNOT FOR FAJIR

Allah hummah dinii fiiman hadait. Wa'aa finii fiiman 'aafait. Watawallanii fiiman tawal-laiit. Wabaariklii fiimaa a'thait. Waqinii birahmatika syarramaa qadhait. Fainnaka taqdhii walaa yuqdha 'alaik. Wainnahu laayadzilu man walait. Walaa ya'izzu man 'aadait. Tabaa rakta rabbanaa wata'aalait. Falakalhamdu 'alaa maaqadhait. Astaghfiruka wa'atuubu ilaik. Wasallallahu 'ala Sayyidina Muhammadin nabiyyil ummiyyi. Wa'alaa aalihi washahbihi Wasallam.

TRANSLATION

O Allah, show me as those You have shown, grant me health as those You have granted health to, take care of me as those You have taken care of, bless me with that which Thou hast bestowed, and deliver me from the harm that Thou hast decreed, for Truly You are the One who judges and is not punished. Therefore, do not dislike those you lead, and do not honor those you despise. Glory be to You and Thee, O our Lord. And may Allah grant mercy and peace to our valued Prophet Muhammad, his family, and his companions in addition to the praises mentioned above. Praise be to You for all the aforementioned praises that You judge.

DUA QOUNT. NAZILAH

Allahummahdiini fiiman hadait. Wa'aafini fiiman 'afait. Watawallanii fiiman tawallait. Wabaarik lii fiima a'thait. Waqinii syarrama qadlait. Fainnaka taqdhi walaa yuqdho 'alaik. Wainnahu laa yadzillu man waalait. Tabaarakta rabbana wata'aalait. astaghfiruka wa atuubu ilaik. Allahummadfa' 'annal ghalaa'a wal balaa'a wabaa'a wal fahsyaa'a wal munkara was suyuufal mukhtalifata wasy syadaa'ida wal mihana maadhahara minhaa wa maabaathana min balaadinaa haadhaaa khaassatan wa min buldaanil muslimiina aammatan. Innaka 'alaa kulli syai'in qadiir. Wa shallallahu 'ala sayyidina muhammadin wa 'ala alihi washahbihi wa shallam.

TRANSLATION:

O Allah, make me one of Your guides among those You lead. Give me salvation among those to whom You have already given it; look after me among those to whom You have already given care; bless me with what You have already given me; shield me from the ugly aspects of what You have chosen; and, undoubtedly, you who decide—it is not decided upon me—will not hate those whom You have protected and assisted. You are supremely holy and high. I beg Your pardon and turn to You in repentance. Allah is our Lord. Save us from the calamities, catastrophes, atrocities, evil, numerous conflicts, brutality, and wars that are apparent and unnoticeable in our nation in particular and the country of the Muslims in general. You truly have control over everything, O Allah. And may Allah pity the loved ones and companions of our revered Prophet Muhammad.

DUAS FOR SUNNAH PRAYER

WHAT IS SUNNAH

The Arabic word for the prophet Muhammad's way of life and legal traditions is sunna. The Qur'an uses the term to refer to the ways of God (Qur'an 33:37, 62) or "ways of life" of prior peoples (Qur'an 3:137), which is a reflection of the pre-Islamic Arab idea of Sunna as the way of life of a tribe.

DUA DHUHA PRAYER

THE BRIGHTNESS OF THE MORNING PRAYER

Allahumma innad-dhuha-a dhuha-uka, wal-baha-a baha-uka, wal-jamala jamaluka, wal-quwwata quwwatuk, wal-qudrata qudratuk, wal-'ismata 'ismatuk. Allahumma in kana rizqi fis-sama-i fa-anzilhu wa-in kana fil-ardhi fa-akhrijhu, wa-in kana ba'eedan faqarribhu, wa-in kana mu'assiran fa yassirhu, wa-in kana haroman fa-tahhirhu, bihaqqi dhuha-ika wa-baha-ika wa jamalika wa quwwatika wa qudratika. Allahumma atini ma ataita 'ibadakas-soliheen

O Allah! The morning's (Dhuha) light is Your radiance, and Your beauty is Your beauty, and Your strength is You might, and Your power is Your power, and Your protection is

Your protection, O Allah. If my food comes from heaven, send it to me; if it comes from the earth, get it out of it for me; if it's far away, bring it closer; if it's difficult, make it easier for me; and if it's banned, cleanse it for me. Please, O Allah, by Your Light, Radiance, Beauty, Might, and Power, gives me what You gave Your righteous slaves.

Importance of Dhuha Prayer:

1. Dhuha is a way for us to express our appreciation to Allah SWT for keeping our bodies healthy. Rasulullah Saw said that the 360 portions of our body that make up each day should be fed with alms. Every man has 360 joints; should each joint's owner make a Sadaqat? Who can achieve that, Ya Rasulullah, the companions then questioned. "Clean up the dirt in the mosque or remove something (that can hurt people) off the highway; if he cannot afford it, then reciting dhuha two rakat can replace it," says Rasulullah SAW.

2. By saying the Dhuha prayer, we can express our desire for Allah SWT to grant us His grace and benefits throughout the day, whether they take the shape of material or physical favors. The sons of Adam, do not ever be sluggish to pray four Rakha's in the morning; it is a praying dhuha, and I will undoubtedly fulfill your necessities till the afternoon," stated Rasulullah SAW.

3. To safeguard oneself from the anguish of hell fire on the day of retribution (the end of the world), one should offer dhuha in prayer. In support of this, the Prophet Muhammad SAW. In his hadith, he states that anyone who does Fajr and then continues to remain in the prayer area during dzikir until the sun rises and then performs prayer in the amount of two rakats will not be prohibited by Allah SWT from having the fire of hell touch or burn his flesh.

4. Allah SWT honors people who pray the dhuha with a recompense from heaven. On the Day of Judgment, a call will be

made asking, where is the one who always offers the dhuha prayer says Rasulullah SAW. In heaven, there is a door known as Bab Adh-Dhuha (Door of Dhuha). Come in with God's love; this is your door.

5. The dhuha award is equal to the hajj and umrah rewards. According to Rasulullah SAW, whoever leaves his home to say the required prayers would receive a reward equivalent to a man performing the Hajj. Anyone who makes the pilgrimage to pray outside will subsequently be rewarded similarly to someone who makes the Umrah.

6. the satisfaction of basic requirements for life Those who enjoy performing dhuha, a sincere prayer to Allah SWT, will find nourishment. Rasulullah SAW explains it in this way. In the Abu Darda qudsi hadith. He said, O Son of Adam, bend (shalatlah) because I am in the early afternoon (Dhuha prayer) four rak'ah; after that, I shall meet (your wants) till the afternoon.

DUA TAHAJJUD (THE NIGHT PRAYER)

Allaahumma Lakal Hamdu Anta
Qayyumus Samaa Waati Wal Ardhi Wa
Man Fiihinna. Wa Lakal Hamdu Anta
Malikus Samaa Waati Wal Ardhi Wa
Man Fiihinna. Wa Lakal Hamdu Anta
Nuurus Samaawaati Wal Ardhi Wa Man
Fiihinna. Wa Lakal Hamdu Antal
Haqqu, Wa Wa'Dukal Haqqu, Wa
Liqaa'Ukal Haqqu, Wa Qaulukal
Haqqun, Wal Jannatu Haqquw
Wannaaru Haqquw Wan-Nabiyyuuna
Haqquw Wa Muhammadun Shallallahu
'Alaihi Wa Sallama Haqquw
Wassaa'Atu Haqq. Allaahumma Laka
Aslamtu Wa Bika Aamantu Wa 'Alaika
Tawakkaltu Wa Ilaika Anabtu. Wa Bika
Khaashamtu Wa Ilaika Haakamtu
Faghfirlii Maa Qoddamtu Wa Maa
Akhkhartu Wa Maa Asrartu Wa Maa
A'Lantu Wa Maa Anta A'Lamu
Bihiminnii Antal Muqoddimu Wa Antal

Mu'Akhkhiru Laa Ilaaha Anta. Wa Laa Haula Wa Laa Quwwata Illaa Billaah.

TRANSLATION

Praise be to Allah, you are the One who looks after the heavens, the earth, and all things within. And you deserve all the glory since you rule over the earth, the skies, and every living thing that inhabits them. And you deserve all the honor because you illuminate the skies, the earth, and everything that resides there. And to You be all glory; You are the Truest; Your word is true; Your meeting is true; Heaven is true; Hell is true; the prophets are true; and the day of Doomsday is a reality. "O Allah, there is no God but You, and there is no power (to avoid disobedience) and no strength (to perform worship) except with Allah's help." "O Allah, to You alone do I surrender, to You alone do I believe, to You alone do I trust, to You alone do I return (to repentance), to You alone do I complain, and to You alone do I ask for a decision."

IMPORTANT OF TAHAJJUD PRAYER:

1. Bring us to a noble and wonderful location by His side. For those who diligently recite the tahajud prayer and honestly hope to receive the Divine's pleasure, Allah SWT has promised to raise His people to a praised location. For millions of pious individuals, attaining an honorable position or a particular place in the eyes of Allah SWT is a desire worth cherishing. The virtuous will be in springs and gardens, taking what their Lord has provided for them. Indeed, they had an excellent reputation earlier. They used to get hardly any sleep at all. They would also beg pardon early in the morning.

2. Deliver hope and prayer. One of the fundamental Sunnah worship practices is tahajud prayer, which is a powerful way for us to communicate with Allah. We can

hope and pray for the future, for the dream of creating a Sakinah family, and for the continual presence of guidance in the tahajud prayer routine. On the third night of the last month, Allah Tabaraka Wa Ta'ala descends (to the world's sky). Whoever calls me, I will grant his appeal, he declared. I will always grant anyone's request. And I pardon anybody who seeks My forgiveness.

3. Become modest. Tahajud prayer, according to Allah SWT, would always be modest and hospitable. We will become modest as a result of the tranquility that reflects inner peace as we go about our daily lives in society. And the servants of the Most Gracious are those who approach the uneducated with a "Peace" greeting while walking on the ground in humility. And those who spend the night kneeling and standing before their Lord.

4. keep one's health Tahajud prayer is without a doubt the most effective medicine for treating a variety of illnesses. As a result, those who are familiar with Tahajud will have a strong immune system and resist illness. Do the night prayer because it has been a custom of pious people before you, a way to draw nearer to Allah, stop sin, undo wrongdoings, and keep all ailments from the body, advised Rasulullah SAW.

5. Keep your beauty or fine looks. Every person must desire attractiveness or an excellent appearance in themselves. A person can get what they want with Tahajud prayer therapy without spending any money at all. The promises of good looks or beauty that come from the Tahajud prayer go beyond the physical appearance at birth. Inner beauty might also result from it. The face of someone who performs numerous night prayers will appear handsome or beautiful during the day, according to Rasulullah SAW.

6. speed up the accomplishment of objectives and a sense of security. We must perform Tahajud prayer in addition to our efforts (ikhtiar), as Allah will grant us everything, we ask for in the prayer that follows Tahajud. Allah will grant us the objectives we desire as well as a sense of security to make life easier. I've given him what he wants (goals) and stability in the face of his concerns.

7. Get rid of your lust and sloth. Laziness and lust can be successfully eliminated with tahajud prayer. We will be better prepared to welcome tomorrow if we complete it at night. Lust is the main foe of man. Tahajud prayer implementation could be a little difficult for some people since it considers the time of work during the hours when we typically go to sleep. At that hour, the urge to retire to bed is undoubtedly quite great. A person who awakens from sleep to do tahajud prayer has thus been able to withstand the urge to worship Allah SWT.

DUA ISTIKHARA (A PRAYER SEEKING GUIDANCE IN MAKING A DECISION.)

Allahumma innee astakheeruka biAAilmik, wa-astaqdiruka biqudratik, wa-as-aluka min fadlikal-AAatheem, fa-innaka taqdiru wala aqdir, wataAAlamu wala aAAlam ,wa-anta AAallamul ghuyoob, allahumma in kunta taAAlamu anna hathal-amr (say your need) khayrun lee fee deenee wamaAAashee waAAaqibati amree faqdurhu lee, wayassirhu lee, thumma barik lee feeh, wa-in kunta taAAlamu anna hathal-amr sharrun lee fee deenee wamaAAashee waAAaqibati amree fasrifhu AAannee wasrifnee AAanh, waqdur liyal-khayra haythu kan, thumma ardinee bih

TRANSLATION

"O Allah, I seek Your guidance by Your knowledge; by Your power, I seek strength; and I implore You from Your immeasurable favor, for You are able while I am not; You are aware while I am not; and You are the Knower of the Unseen. O Allah, if You know this matter—and he mentions his need here—to be beneficial for me in terms of my religion, my life, and my end, then decree and make it possible for me, and bless me with it; and if You know this matter to be detrimental to my religion, my life, and my end, then remove it from me and remove me from it, and decree for me what is beneficial wherever it may be, and make me satisfied with such.

ALHAMDULILLAH

www.ingramcontent.com/pod-product-compliance
Lightning Source LLC
Chambersburg PA
CBHW070418220526
45466CB00004B/1457